ZEBRA'S HICCUPS

For Satoshi and Yoko

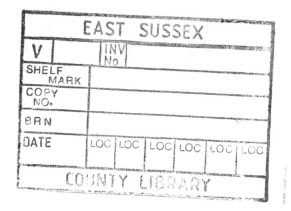
A Red Fox Book

Published by Random House Children's Books
20 Vauxhall Bridge Road, London SW1V 2SA

A division of Random House UK Ltd.
London Melbourne Sydney Auckland
Johannesburg and agencies throughout the world

First published by Andersen Press Ltd 1991

Red Fox edition 1993

Printed in Hong Kong

ISBN 0 09 918381 1

ZEBRA'S HICCUPS
DAVID McKEE

RED FOX

The animals loved to play.
"Come and play, Zebra," they called. "This is fun."
"No thank you, I am busy," Zebra answered. He was a
very serious and dignified zebra.

One day, Zebra got hiccups.
"Oh my, how extremely inconvenient HIC," he said to
himself. "I shall simply, HIC, ignore them and go out for
a walk. Perhaps they will disappear.

"Hi there, Zebra," said Tiger.
"Good HIC, ah. Good morning HIC," said Zebra.
"Hiccups!" said Tiger. "Don't worry I know a cure.
  Hold your breath, close your eyes, and say the
  alphabet backwards."
"That sounds much too HIC silly," said Zebra.

"Yoo hoo, Zebra," called Miss Pig. "Come skating with me."

"Good morning Miss P HIC," said Zebra.

"Hiccups?" asked Miss Pig. "I know a great cure. Put your head between your knees and drink a glass of water upside down."

"No HIC you," said Zebra. "That is far too un-HIC dignified for me."

"Zebra's got hiccups," said Little Elephant. "When I get hiccups I stand on one leg and go, 'too d'loo d'loo d'loo d'loo,' as long as I can."

"Me too," grinned Big Elephant.

"But definitely not me, HIC," said Zebra.

Next Zebra met Crocodile.

"Shoot baskets with me," said Crocodile.

"No, thank you Croco HIC," said Zebra.

"Oh-oh, who has hiccups?" said Crocodile. "Here's a sure fire hicketty cure. Stand on your head, hold the ball between your legs and sing. Clicketty, click. Works every time."

"I'm sure," said Zebra. "HIC."

Then, something strange began to happen. The hiccuping began to move Zebra's stripes. The more he hiccuped the more his stripes bumped together. Zebra never noticed.

It was Mrs Duck who told him.
"Is that you Zebra?" she said. "You do look strange."
"You mean HIC sound strange," said Zebra. "It's hiccups."
"I mean look strange. Look at yourself," said Mrs Duck.

"OH NO," groaned Zebra. "Just look what has happened. I look HICdiculous. My wonderful stripes."

"I should have tried the cures," said Zebra. "What was it that Tiger said? I can't remember HIC."
He hurried back to find Tiger.

At Tiger's, Zebra took a deep breath, closed his eyes and said, "ZYXV no W HIC. Oh dear, HIC I mean ZYXWVUT HIC RS NO SR HIC."

Tiger chuckled and Zebra opened his eyes.
"This will never work," he sighed. "I'm off to try Miss
Pig's HIC. It's not funny you HIC know."
"I think it's very funny," said Tiger. "Wait for me."

Miss Pig gave Zebra a glass of water and said, "Head between your knees and drink this upside down." Zebra sat and drank and coughed and spluttered and choked and finally hiccuped.

"HIC. Absolutely HICely hopeless, and very HIC messy,"
said Zebra with a little smile. "Let's try Elephant's cure."

"I'll help you Zebra," said Little Elephant. "Stand on one leg and 'too d'loo d'loo d'loo' as long as you can." Zebra went "too d'loo d'HIC d'loo d'loo HIC loo d'loo HIC," until the others laughed.

Zebra grinned. "Totally useless. Come on HIC. Maybe HICodile's clicketty cure can stop these hicketty HICcups."

"First a headstand," said Crocodile. "Ball between your legs. Now sing."
Zebra just laughed and so did all the others.

"It doesn't work if you laugh," giggled Crocodile.
"I can't help HIC, it," said Zebra, and he fell over still
laughing.

Mrs Duck came along to see what all the noise was about.
"He can't HIC for ever," she said.
Then, keeping her voice low so that Zebra wouldn't hear,
she told the others what to do.

Zebra was recovering from laughing when he was
drenched by cold water.
"Now that's not funny," he said. "Not funny at all." But
there was not one HIC.

"The shock has worked! He's cured," said Mrs Duck.
"Hooray," shouted all the animals.
"But I do feel strange without my stripes," said Zebra.

The cold water made him shiver. Then he sneezed a huge sneeze. The sneeze did the trick. It shook the stripes back into place. "Two cures in one," said Zebra. "Thank you all."

"You've caught a chill," said Tiger. "I know a great cure."
"So do I, so do I," the others all shouted together.
"And so do I," laughed Zebra as he waved goodbye to
his friends.
"I wonder what we'll play tomorrow?" he thought as
he hurried home to a hot bath, a hot drink and a nice
warm bed . . .

Some bestselling Red Fox picture books

THE BIG ALFIE AND ANNIE ROSE STORYBOOK
by Shirley Hughes
OLD BEAR
by Jane Hissey
OI! GET OFF OUR TRAIN
by John Burningham
I WANT A CAT
by Tony Ross
NOT NOW, BERNARD
by David McKee
ALL JOIN IN
by Quentin Blake
THE SAND HORSE
by Michael Foreman and Ann Turnbull
BAD BORIS GOES TO SCHOOL
by Susie Jenkin-Pearce
BILBO'S LAST SONG
by J.R.R. Tolkien
MATILDA
by Hilaire Belloc and Posy Simmonds
WILLY AND HUGH
by Anthony Browne
THE WINTER HEDGEHOG
by Ann and Reg Cartwright
A DARK, DARK TALE
by Ruth Brown
HARRY, THE DIRTY DOG
by Gene Zion and Margaret Bloy Graham
DR XARGLE'S BOOK OF EARTHLETS
by Jeanne Willis and Tony Ross
JAKE
by Deborah King